I AM ME!!

EM.EM Genesis

I AM ME!!

My name is LIONEL.

I AM ME!!

BY

EM.EM.GENESIS 2012

www.booksbyememgenesis.com

This book belongs to:

Name:

Age:

I AM ME!!

I AM ME!!

PUBLISHED BY:

EM.EM.GENESIS

WWW.BOOKSBYEMEMGENESIS.COM

I AM ME!!

My name is Lionel and I am 7 years old. Apart from my Dad, I am the only male in our house.

I AM ME!!

I have two sisters, Stephanie and Serena. My Mom also lives with us.

My Mom tells me often that I am the cutest boy ever.

I have really big hair.

I AM ME!!

Grandma calls it Afro. She says it makes me look so cute, and handsome.

When I comb my hair, it stands up by itself. It is silky, soft and shiny. I take good care of my Afro. I agree with my grandma, my Afro makes me look handsome and unique. I love my Afro!!

My skin is brown like chocolate, smooth and shiny.

Mommy tells me that I am perfectly made.

I AM ME!!

I AM ME!!

My Dad says that I look like him,

because I have his beautiful ebony skin.

I AM ME!!

I like that I look like my dad, but, when I see my Mom, I think I look like her too.

I'm Brown and Ebony, just like my parents and my Sisters. I like myself.

I AM ME!!

I AM ME!!

Although many kids in my class don't look like me, my Teacher tells me all the time that, I'm adorable, and, smart.

She knows I want to be a Doctor when I grow up, so, she encourages me, and,

even bought me a   stethoscope last Christmas.

I took it home, and, showed it to my family.

I AM ME!!

My Dad lets me use the stethoscope to listen to his heartbeat once, and, I could hear his heart beating really loud, and fast. This made me laugh.

I haven't decided yet what type of Doctor I would like to be when I grow up. Maybe I'll be a children's Doctor.

My Sister Stepanie told me that children' Doctors are called Paediatrician. I couldn't pronounce that word at first but I practiced it until I was able to pronounce it.

I didn't give up, because,

I AM ME!!

One day, I may become a Paediatrician, or maybe a Heart Surgeon, like my Dad.

Stephanie wants to be a Dentist when she grows up.

She's always trying to put metal

instruments inside my mouth to check my teeth.

I AM ME!!

I run away from her because and I'm scared of Dentists.

My sister Serena wants to be a Dancer. She teaches me different types of dance moves, including ballet.

I like to dance too.

I AM ME!!

I AM ME!!

I have an idea, I think I'll become a dancing Paediatrician. Hmmmm... I thought to myself.

A dancing Doctor would be fun, and, different to other types of Doctors.

I could dance, and, make sick children smile, then still give them some medicine so they can feel healthier.

I like being different.

I AM ME!!

I AM ME!!

My Grandad likes to pinch my nose playfully. He tells me that I have the cutest nose ever. But sometimes, I don't think so, because when I get a cold, I have to blow through my nose, and, that hurts me. When it hurts, my nose does not feel or look cute, but, I guess most times when I don't have a cold,my nose looks cute. I believe my grandad when he tells me I have the cutest nose.

I AM ME!!

I AM ME!!

My Mom's friend, Aunty Tia calls me *birdeyes*. She says it's because I have beautiful, big, brown eyes, and I stare a lot. Aunty is beautiful too.

Aunty Tia has very long legs and she's very tall.

Mommy said she's a lawyer like her, and, she wins many of her cases.

I like it when she calls me birdeyes because,

I AM ME!!

I have friends with different skin shades, and, we all play together.

I AM ME!!

Some are friends from school, and, some are from my neighborhood.

I have one best friend! Although, my best friend, Brian has a different skin color to mine, and, different hair, but, it doesn't bother us at all, because, we love ourselves just as we are.

Our parents are friends, and Brian's Mom always tells us that God made people of different shades, and, colors, and, that we're all beautiful, because, we all look just like God. I wonder if Brian's Mom had seen God before, or how did she know what God looks like?

I believe Brian's Mom. Maybe we all look like God.

I like all my friends anyway, and they all like me too. Some of us go to the same school, and, some of us attend the same class.

During play time, we play football, and, I often stop the ball from going into the goal post. So, my friends tease me, and call me, "The Stopper."

I just shrug my shoulders, say thank you to my friends, and smile because,

I AM ME!!

One time, we had a spelling competition, but, my team was a few points down.

We had to spell

"Buckingham Palace". I remembered how to spell it because my parents once took us to London, England to visit the Palace.

I AM ME!!

Although, we didn't see the Queen of England, but, I never forgot how to spell Buckingham Palace.

I pressed the buzzer quickly, held my breath for a few seconds then I spelled; "B-U-C-K-I-N-G-H-A-M P-A-L-A-C-E."

The room was silent at first, but then everybody applauded, because it was the correct answer. I was happy that my team won the Spelling competition. We each got red medals for our win.

We were the champions!! I felt like a champion, especially after I placed my

I AM ME!!

medaI around my neck. I enjoy reading and, I'm very good at spelling.

I study hard, and, I like to be smart, so, I could be a Doctor when I grow up. Daddy always tells my sister and me, that, the only way we will be successful at anything we try to do, is by learning, practicing, and, working hard.

He often tells us that, 'Practice makes Perfect!'

So, I listen to my dad, and, I practiced and, worked hard in all my exams, and, I always get top marks in school.

I AM ME!!

I AM ME!!

When it comes to food, I like to eat all sorts of food and fruits, except bananas.

My parents tell me that if I eat well, I will grow up to be healthy, and, strong but, there's one fruit I've never liked, and, that is a Banana.

My Dad said I've never liked bananas, even as a baby.

I AM ME!!

Sometimes, my friends laugh at me, especially as I make faces, when they try to force me to eat a banana, but, I always refuse to eat it.

I didn't mind being the odd one out who didn't like bananas, so when they tease me about not liking bananas, I simply shrugged my shoulders and say to myself:

I AM ME!!

I AM ME!!

Every time I talk to a girl named Shelley, my friends make fun of us, and call her my girlfriend.

I don't get upset about it, because my Mom always told me that I was too young to have a serious girlfriend.

I AM ME!!

Daddy also tells me that if I had a girlfriend, I would have to take her out to eat, and, take her to the movies. So, I have decided to wait until I'm old enough to have a job, and, then I can take a girl out on a date.

But for now, Shelley and me, are just friends.

When I told my friends that Shelley and me were just friends, they pointed at me laughed, and, kept calling her my girlfriend. We all laughed about it, then, I chased them around the school.

I AM ME!!

When they continued to laugh at me about Shelley, I simply shrugged my shoulders, smiled and thought to myself:

I AM ME!!

Although, I have many friends, I have learned to be self-disciplined, and, I do do everything my friends do. Mommy always teaches us to dare to be different, and, think without limits.

She tells my sisters and me all the time, "I want you to always be yourselves, and, not what other people

I AM ME!!

want you to be." I try to listen to my parents most times.

I like myself. My lovely, ebony shade, my big Afro hair which stands tall when I comb it, my big brown eyes... like birdeyes, and, my cute, small nose.

I love myself, because, there is only one of me in the entire Universe.

I AM ME!!

I AM ME!!

I AM ME!!

NOTES:

THE END.

WWW.BOOKSBYEMEMGENESIS.COM

I AM ME!!

Other Book Titles by EM.EM.Genesis:

- CECILIA & THE BUMBLEBEES IN English, German, Spanish, Italian, French
- CECILIA & THE BUMBLEBEES
- I AM..
- I AM ME!!
- NO!! ABIGAIL!!
- SUPER DUPER RIH SAVES THE DAY
- CALL ME MADAM BOSS
- CECILIA & THE SCARY SANTA
- ANANIA GOES TO…
- ANANIA GOES TO…AFRICA

I AM ME!!

I AM ME! by EM.EM.Genesis is a great book for Pre-school to First Grade kids.

Seven Year old Lionel enjoys playing with his friends and loves his family but most importantly, he has learned to love himself.
Lionel wants to be a Dancing Doctor when he grows up.
Lionel doesn't allow much to bother him because he's a happy-go-lucky lad and even when his friends make fun of him sometimes, he just smiles and says:
"I AM ME!

I AM ME!!

EM.EM Genesis

Made in the USA
Middletown, DE
12 January 2023

21947470R00022